For
Malachy Doyle
—M. R.

MEADOW
FRESH

IS HE LESS THAN
FRAGRANT AND
GRUBBY AROUND
THE EARS?

AQUAPHOBIC
DRY
SHAMPOO

ELBOW
GREASE

Washing a woolly
mammoth can
be hard work.

TUSK
WHITENER

ANTIBACTERIAL
HOOF
WASH

curl
tamer

TANGLES BE GONE!
Use liberally for
best results.

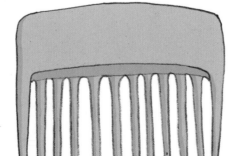

SOAP

To my
grandparents
—K. H.

HOW TO WASH A
WOOLLY
MAMMOTH

MICHELLE ROBINSON · KATE HINDLEY

HENRY HOLT AND COMPANY
New York

Does your woolly mammoth need a bath?
You'll need to prepare!

Woolly mammoths are quite BIG,
and wool is notoriously tricky to clean.
Don't worry, just follow this step-by-step guide.

Fill the bath tub.

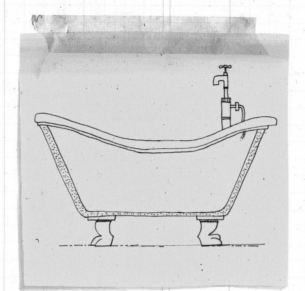

Fig. 1: Empty

Fig. 2: Full

If your mammoth is thirsty, this may take a while.

STEP TWO:
Add bubble bath.

STEP THREE:
Add mammoth.

Fig. 1: Broom

Fig. 2: Spooky mask

Fig. 3: Skateboard

Fig. 4: Heavy-duty crane

When all else fails,
there is always cake.

STEP FOUR:
Start scrubbing.
Don't forget to wash
behind those ears!

STEP FIVE:
Wash his big, fat tummy.

CAREFUL!
A mammoth's tummy is terribly tickly.

STEP SIX:
   Open an umbrella
   and stand back!

STEP SEVEN:
Now for the really hairy bit.

You're going to need some shampoo—not too much!

Fig. 1:
Bubble bliss

Fig. 2:
Who me?

Fig. 3:
Hair-raising

Fig. 4:
Mammoth mullet

Fig. 5:
And that is?

Fig. 6:
Twirly-whirly

Fig. 7:
The King

Fig. 8:
Comb-over

Be CAREFUL

not to get any in

the mammoth's . . .

Oh, dear.

STEP EIGHT:
To get a wet woolly mammoth down from a tree, you'll need . . . .

. . . a very STRONG trampoline.

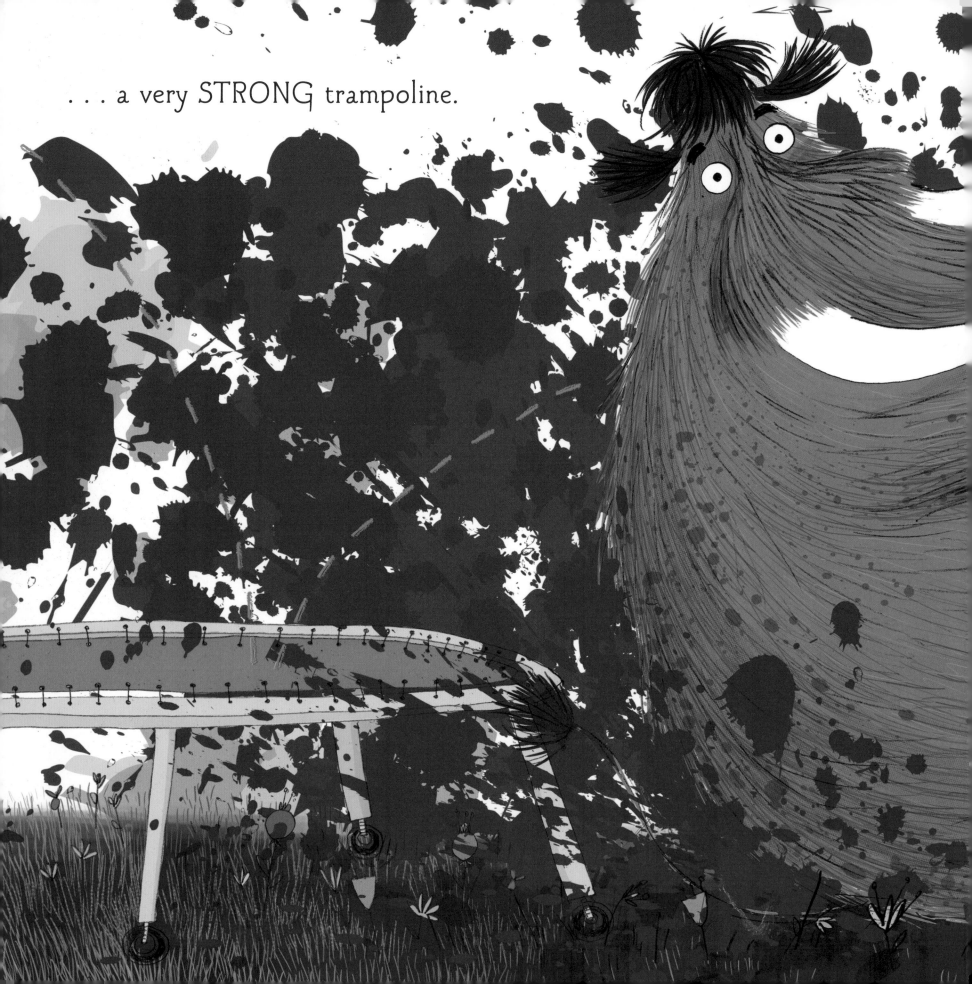

STEP NINE:

Let him share a bath with YOU!

STEP TEN:

Throw in the towel

and SNUGGLE!

Henry Holt and Company, LLC
Publishers since 1866
175 Fifth Avenue
New York, New York 10010
mackids.com

Library of Congress Cataloging-in-Publication Data
Robinson, Michelle (Michelle Jane).
How to wash a woolly mammoth / Michelle Robinson, Kate Hindley. —
First American edition.
pages   cm
Originally published in the United Kingdom
by Simon and Schuster UK Ltd., 2013.
Summary: "Follow this step-by-step guide to successfully clean up your hairy
friend. But be forewarned. A mammoth's tummy is terribly tickly"
—Provided by publisher.
ISBN 978-0-8050-9966-9 (hardback)
[1. Woolly mammoth—Fiction. 2. Baths—Fiction. 3. Humorous stories.]
I. Hindley, Kate, illustrator. II. Title.
PZ7.R567535Ho 2014   [E]—dc23   2013030800

Henry Holt books may be purchased for business or promotional use.
For information on bulk purchases, please contact Macmillan Corporate and
Premium Sales Department at (800) 221-7945 x5442 or
by e-mail at specialmarkets@macmillan.com.

First published in hardcover in 2013 by Simon and Schuster UK Ltd.
First American edition—2014
Printed in China by Toppan Leefung Printing,
Dongguan City, Guangdong Province.

1   3   5   7   9   10   8   6   4   2